CRYSTALS, CAULDRONS, AND CRIME

Deepwood Witches Mysteries
Novella

Shéa MacLeod

Sunwalker
Press

CHAPTER ONE

Edwina Gale was a witch set in her ways. Having those ways disrupted was a good way to make her... testy. And this morning, Edwina Gale was extremely testy.

She tapped one booted foot against the sidewalk and glared at the glass door of Pink Lady Donuts as if staring at it long enough would make it magically open. Maybe it would. She had powers, after all, although they ran more to tracking killers than opening doors. But this was an emergency situation – she was in dire need of a donut. And not just any donut. Virgil's maple bacon bars. Only...

Virgil Zante was nowhere in sight.

She crossed her arms and grumbled, "Where are you, Virgil?"

Virgil didn't answer. The store — painted a color somewhere in between that stomach-easing goop and bubble gum — was still dark. Worst of all, the air was fresh and clean with the faint hint of petrichor from the morning's rain. Normally something she'd find pleasing but, in this instance, it pissed her off. The air should be redolent with the scents of yeasty dough and caramelized sugar. It was six in the freaking morning. Where was Virgil?

Edwina had lived in Deepwood, Oregon nearly twenty years now, ever since she'd retired from the military and decided she wanted a slower pace of life. That had been the same year Virgil had opened his donut shop. It had been a match made in heaven. She'd never missed a morning in all those twenty years and neither had he.

Until today.

A heavy feeling of unease crept over the irritation, turning it to anxiety. This wasn't like Virgil. At all.

"Don't be daft, woman," she muttered. "He probably went on vacation."

Except Virgil hadn't gone on vacation as long as she'd known him. Maybe he was sick? Nope, he'd never been sick, either. And that one time he'd had his appendix out, his husband, David, took over for a couple days. Personally, she'd thought Virgil should take off more than a couple days, but what did she know? Her appendix was still rattling around in there. Probably petrified by now.

By this time her witch senses were screaming at her until the back of her neck itched with it. Something was wrong, only she wasn't sure what to do about it. Yet.

Another few minutes ticked by, and still no Virgil. She was just about to hunt him down when her phone rang. She'd have ignored it, except it was her diner. She'd thought it would be fun to run a diner in her retirement, so she'd bought a local joint called Norma's and started baking pies. Joke was on her. "Retiring" wasn't something anyone did in the supernatural community. The minute she'd moved to Deepwood, the local witch council had put her to work as a sort of paranormal enforcer to secretly aid the police force which was comprised completely of mundane humans — those without knowledge of the magical world and its denizens.

Until recently anyway. There was a new sheriff in town, so to speak, and he knew all about witches and shifters and magic and such. But that was another story.

She answered on the third ring. "Yes?"

"Hey, Edwina, got a bit of an emergency here." It was Maisie, the normally unflappable waitress at Norma's Diner. Her tone was definitely... flapped.

6

Edwina inhaled deeply. "What is the nature of the emergency?" She sounded like one of those emergency operators. She blamed lack of donuts.

"There's a naked guy. Like completely naked. He insists on being served and refuses to leave. I'm going to have to bleach the heck out of the bar stool."

Because of course there was a naked guy. "Why don't you call the cops? That's what they're there for."

"Because he says he'll hex anyone who touches him." Maisie lowered her voice. "That could get sticky; know what I mean?"

She did. Her job was to prevent things like naked guys hexing police. Chances were he was an ordinary mortal with a penchant for letting it all hang out and a disrespect of other people's space, but if he actually had the power to put a hex on people, well, that could be a big problem. And it was her problem to solve.

Yay, her.

She sighed. "Be there in five." And without her donut.

That naked guy was going to lose his donuts.

The guy sitting at the Formica counter was, indeed, totally, completely naked. He was also as scrawny as an underfed chicken and as wrinkled as a raisin. He'd spread his legs so his donut holes were neatly spread out over the barstool.

Forget bleach. She'd have to burn the place down.

She recognized the man from the neighborhood. Like her, he was a fan of Virgil's donuts, although he preferred the double chocolate with raspberry dust.

Maisie peered out from the pass-through to the kitchen. Her husband — who was also the diner's cook — stared over her shoulder. Fabulous.

Breakfast and a show. She turned to her current problem.

"How's it hanging, Fred?" She considered circling the counter to put some distance between herself and Fred, but then she figured she'd probably better block the view of his business from the rest of the diners.

Fred glanced up and gave her a toothless grin. He'd forgotten his dentures again. "Hey, Edwina. It's hanging." He glanced at his lap and burst into laughter. "It's hanging just fine."

Fred was basically harmless. He talked to himself a lot and tended to wear fewer clothes than most people considered appropriate, but as far as she knew, he didn't have the ability to hex anyone.

"Why are you naked, Fred?"

He squared his stooped shoulders as best he could. "I was born this way, and this is the way I'm going out."

"Are you going out today?"

He frowned. "Well, it's hard to say now. It is a full moon coming up."

She'd forgotten. Well, not forgotten so much as hadn't remembered. Things had been a bit hectic lately. Full moon was in two days and Mabon was two after that. "Sure. What's that got to do with you sitting at my counter without a stitch on?"

"Had my palm read once. Said I'd go out on a full moon. Might be today. Thought I'd get some pie first."

"Sure, but you do know you have to wear clothes."

"I do not! No place in the city ordinance is it illegal to be naked."

A migraine pounded behind her temples. "You got me there, Fred. However, the health inspector would disagree with that notion."

"Health inspector ain't here." Fred crossed his arms.

"But I am, and I reserve the right to refuse service to anyone. Go home and put some shorts on. Then you can come have pie," she said in a tone that made most people quail.

His jaw jutted out. "Ain't going nowhere. I got rights."

"You see all these customers here?" There were two customers, and both were trying hard not to look at Fred. One had sunk down in his booth, and the other was hiding behind her cell phone. Good luck with that. "They got rights, too. They got the right not to have to see your shriveled gonads while they're eating."

"I'll put a hex on you!" Fred threatened.

She narrowed her eyes. "I'd like to see you try."

He mumbled something under his breath.

She lifted one iron gray eyebrow. "Try again."

"All right. I'll go. But I'm coming back for pie."

"That's fine. As long as you have clothes on."

He sauntered out the door, waving in the breeze, muttering about freedom and fascists. She'd like to show him fascists. Her dad fought fascists in Europe during World War II. Fighting fascists was in her blood.

Maisie appeared around the pie case, a roll of paper towels in one hand and a bottle of bleach in the other. Yellow rubber gloves were hiked up to her elbows and she wore a face mask and the goggles Jupiter the cook used when he chopped onions.

Edwina rolled her eyes. "You can bleach it if you want to, but it's getting replaced." No way could she let other patrons sit there after Fred's donut holes were all over it. No amount of bleach could ever get rid of that image.

Maisie heaved a sigh of relief. "Thank goodness. I'm still bleaching it though. And then I'm bleaching my brain."

"I might join you," Edwina said. Because if this was what this month's full moon was going to be like, she wanted nothing to do with it. Especially without her morning donut.

Where the blazes was Virgil?

Crystals, Cauldrons, and Crime

CHAPTER
TWO

"You look nice, Edwina." Chief Jeremiah Dekes' voice was a low Sam Elliott rumble of admiration. It matched his lanky frame, white hair, and flourishing moustache.

"Thanks. You look pretty good yourself." She might be over the six-decade mark, but she wasn't totally immune to flattery. Especially from Jeremiah Dekes.

They'd met a few months earlier when he'd stolen her morning donuts. Not being one to settle for anything other than Virgil's maple bacon bars,

15

she'd tracked him down and demanded her donuts back. The rest, as they say, was history.

Unlike every other Chief of Police Deepwood had ever had, Dekes was well aware of things supernatural even though he had no magic himself. According to him, his stepfather had been a shifter. Which meant he knew about the paranormal world hidden right under the noses of mundane humans. And once she knew that he knew about such things, she no longer had to hide magical crime scenes from him, although they did still have to keep things under wraps when it came to the rest of the department and half of the citizenry.

Deepwood was one of those strange towns where the magical mixed with the mundane – only somehow the mundane never even knew it. It always seemed to her like a smart person would figure things out, but she'd noticed that non-magical humans tended to gloss over anything that didn't fit in their world view. And witches, shifters, gargoyles, vampires, and so on definitely didn't fit into most people's world view.

"Stop by Pink Lady lately?" She kept her tone light, as if she were teasing him over their shared donut obsession. Just in case anyone was listening in. Not that anyone was. Luna Cafe was the sort of place one brought someone special for a romantic meal, not for eavesdropping. Which was probably why Jeremiah had brought her here.

"This morning, only the shop was closed." He sliced off a piece of steak and popped it in his mouth. From his ecstatic eyeroll, it must have been good.

Luna Café was owned by a kitchen witch, who was also the chef. The food was beyond magic.

She tried her blue cheese and mushroom gnocchi. It was savory and rich. Pure heaven. "You don't find that... strange?"

Jeremiah eyed her, obviously realizing that her question wasn't as casual as she'd made it sound. "Should I?"

She shrugged, taking a sip of wine. "Not sure. It's just that Pink Lady hasn't been closed a single day since Virgil opened shop. He's obsessive like that. He wouldn't just... not open."

"Emergency?"

"He'd have gotten his husband David to take over."

Jeremiah chewed thoughtfully. "Maybe whatever emergency it was involved David, too."

"I suppose. But in that case, he'd have definitely left a note on the door. Virgil considers himself responsible to his customers."

Jeremiah nodded. "Interesting. Don't know that it means anything though."

"I know. He's a grown man. He has the right not to open his donut shop."

He laid a hand atop hers. It was warm, comforting. He had a soothing quality about him that she enjoyed more than she ever thought she would. "But you're worried."

"Yes. I am. It doesn't feel right."

"You want me to look into it?" There was no judgement in his tone. No sign he thought she was being ridiculous or dramatic.

The fact he believed her, well, it shouldn't have surprised her, but it did. She was used to men questioning her authority. Most just saw a cantankerous old lady with strange fashion sense and brushed her off. They didn't know she could kill them with a ballpoint pen. In fact, she could kill them with a feather if she put her mind to it.

"Thank you, but I think I should handle it for now. No sense calling in the big guns until I know there's something wrong."

He laughed. "You are the big guns, Edwina."

She winked. "And don't you forget it."

The next morning Edwina headed to Pink Lady with some trepidation. She hadn't slept well, but unfortunately not for fun reasons.

Jeremiah had been called away in the middle of dessert thanks to some emergency at the police station. Apparently a woman had called screaming that there was a rock on her lawn.

A rock.

Full moon madness was starting early.

She'd never bought into the theory until she and Jeremiah started seeing each other. The stories he told were so bat guano crazy, she'd first thought he was making them up to entertain her. Until she googled the incidents. He hadn't been making anything up.

After they'd left the restaurant, she'd driven by Pink Lady. Granted, it was well past closing hour, but there was no sign it had ever been open. A UPS package that had been left by the door was still there, and the trash bins around back were empty even though it wasn't garbage day. It gave her a bad feeling.

All night that feeling had intensified, crawling up and over her scalp, itching between her shoulder blades. She'd tossed and turned, catching nothing more than cat naps here and there in between bouts of worry. She hadn't been this angsty since she'd finished menopause nearly a decade ago. Oh, sure, she had rough nights now and then, but more often than not she slept like the dead.

A shiver ran up her spine. Maybe she shouldn't think about death what with Virgil missing and all.

Trepidation turned to stomach churning queasiness as she found the lights still out and the door locked. The UPS package sat in the exact same spot. Once again, the air lacked the usual scent of frying donuts. Not a good sign. Where the blue blazes was Virgil?

She glanced up and down Main Street as if he might pop out of an alley or from behind one of the decorative planters that lined the street. No such luck, but a slightly swaying sign caught her attention. It bore the image of a wolf howling at the moon.

Her purple broomstick skirt swooshed about her matching Doc Martens as she marched the block and a half to Howling Moon Cafe. It was run by Flynn and Charis Faolan. He was half sidhe and she was supposedly non-magical, although she'd been part of the supernatural community in her native Greece. Interesting match, but it worked for them. Their coffee shop was almost as popular as Pink Lady, though their focus, besides coffee, was muffins, scones, and other typical coffee shop fare.

The bell above the door jangled as she pushed her way inside. The scent of roasted coffee beans shot straight up her nose, jarring her awake. She stopped and inhaled again, deeply, intently. Coffee beans were pure magic, and she'd fight anyone who said different.

"Hey, Edwina," Charis sang from behind the counter. Her smooth, dark hair was done up in warrior braids and her sidhe mating tattoo was exposed by a gold tank top which set off her bronze skin. She was gorgeous, like a young Irene Papas. "What can I get you?"

"Caramel macchiato." She'd had enough of drinking cheap black coffee in the military. Give her all the floof all the time. "And a cherry chocolate muffin." It wasn't a donut, but it would have to do.

"You got it. Surprised you're not carrying your usual pink box." Charis's tone was teasing.

"Yeah, well, Pink Lady is closed."

Charis paused. Her dark eyes widened. "Closed?"

"Weird, right?"

"Super weird." She went back to fiddling with the fancy coffee machine. "Virgil never closes."

"That's what I said. But here's where it gets real hinky. He was closed yesterday, too."

Charis turned slowly toward her. "That can't be right."

"But it is. Shop's closed. No sign he was there at all yesterday."

"And no David?"

"No David."

Charis finished up with the coffee and put it on the counter along with a muffin from the case. She frowned as she rang up Edwina's order. "That worries me."

"Me, too," Edwina admitted. "He didn't say anything to you on Friday?"

"No, he didn't. We were pretty busy that day. I waved to him when I was putting the A-frame sign out, but other than that..."

"And he closes before you do," Edwina mused.

Charis nodded. "By the time we shut up shop and walked home, Pink Lady was already closed." She bit her lip. "Something weird happened that morning though."

Edwina took a sip of her coffee. Definitely magic. She wondered what Flynn had put in it. Something extra jazzy from the feel. It gave her a bit of... zip. "What was that?"

"Flynn came in late that day. Had to park in front of Pink Lady because the spot in front of our shop was full and he was carrying a bunch of stuff. Anyway, Virgil comes busting out of his shop and yells at Flynn for parking in front of Pink Lady instead of Howling Moon. It was..."

"Out of character," Edwina supplied.

"Completely."

Virgil was the most even-keeled person Edwina had ever met. Even when she was in her foulest mood, he always had a smile and a kind word. Nothing ever seemed to ruffle him, and yet he'd gotten in a fight with a sidhe over a public parking space?

"What the devil is going on?" she muttered.

"I don't know, but I'll tell you one thing," Charis said. "I will be glad when this full moon business is over."

CHAPTER

THREE

Since it was Sunday and typically slow other than the brief after-church rush, it was Maisie's day off, which meant Edwina was the only waitress. As much as she wanted to get on the hunt for Virgil, she had a business to run. Fortunately, the witch council didn't have her working on any assignments, so she didn't have to deal with that. On the upside, the coven came in at eleven for their usual brunch get-together.

Deepwood had three covens. Most of the witches with real supernatural powers belonged to the big one. The mundanes, who followed wicca and claimed to believe in magic but had never seen actual power, made up a second smaller one. Then there was the one almost nobody knew about. The coven made up of four special witches with incredible power. Witches she considered friends.

Although a witch herself, Edwina wasn't technically part of a coven – and she liked it that way. She was a solitary practitioner. Still, she enjoyed the company of certain other witches from time to time. Particularly this coven.

"Morning, Edwina!" Emory Chastain was a spellwalker, a witch who could literally see spells and walk through them, tweaking them like they were physical entities until they suited her needs. Her strawberry blonde hair was piled on her head, and she wore a flowing turquoise dress that complimented her blue eyes.

"Fine, thanks." Edwina poured her a cup of coffee without being asked. She knew how these witches rolled.

Veri Leveau gave Edwina a sideways glance, her dark eyes glittering with knowledge that always made Edwina a tad uncomfortable. She wore a bright yellow jumpsuit that brought out the gold in her brown skin. "Sure about that?"

Edwina snorted, filling Veri's mug. "Not entirely, but there's not much you can do about it."

"Try us." Lene—pronounced Len-ah—leaned forward, nearly dipping her blonde curls into her freshly poured coffee. She'd swapped out her usual pink cat's eyeglasses for rhinestone studded red ones that matched her Wonder Woman tee-shirt.

Edwina glanced at the fourth and final member of their group. Mia was the youngest and quietest, but there was a calm confidence in her that Edwina was pleased to see. It hadn't always been so.

She heaved a sigh. "Fine then. A friend of mine's gone missing. Virgil."

Lene's eyes widened. "The donut guy?"

"What happened?" Veri interrupted her sister witch.

Edwina shrugged. "No idea. Just hasn't shown up for work the last couple of days. I'm... concerned. It's very unlike him."

Emory nodded. "I get that, but maybe he went on vacation or something?"

Edwina gritted her teeth, annoyed at having to go over things yet again. She really should just handle things herself. She was about to say so when Mia, of all people, spoke up.

"You're right to be concerned." Her eyes had taken on a faraway look they got sometimes. Mia was a dreamwalker, which meant visions. Usually when she was asleep, but sometimes they happened even while she was awake.

Edwina knew Mia had been practicing her craft, learning to tap into those visions on purpose instead of letting them take over her. It wasn't an easy road, though. By nature, dreamwalker witches tended to go doolally a bit young, thanks to the fact that they couldn't control the visions. In the old days, mental institutions had been full of them. These days, the few that were left were mostly medicated into oblivion.

"What do you mean?" Edwina asked.

"It's the full moon." Mia's tone held a hint of dreaminess. "They always disappear near the full moon."

"Who does?" Emory demanded.

"Shifters," Mia said.

"Virgil isn't a shifter," Edwina protested. Although, actually, she had no idea what he was. She knew he was... something. But he never said, and she didn't ask. She always figured if a person wanted her to know personal details about themselves, they'd tell her. But his energy wasn't shifter-like. It was… different. Like nothing she'd ever experienced before.

"Isn't he?" Mia said dreamily.

"Doesn't matter. He's disappeared," Edwina said. "Do you know where? Why?"

Mia shook her head, inky hair sliding over her shoulders. "But I do know one thing."

"What?" Edwina and the other three witches demanded in unison.

"They never come back."

They never come back.

All day Mia's words had haunted Edwina until she thought she might jump out of her skin. She wanted nothing more than to get on the trail. She needed to find Virgil before it was too late.

Too late for what, though, was anyone's guess. Mia had told them that for the last several full moons, shifters had been going missing. Most of them were people without families to worry about them and so had gone under the radar. She'd had no idea where they'd gone, if they'd been taken (or left of their own free will), or why. Only that they'd disappeared and never come back. For all she knew they could be in Boca Raton soaking up the sun.

Although Edwina seriously doubted that.

Mia had also been unable to explain why Virgil, who wasn't a shifter – probably – had disappeared or if he was for sure connected to the other disappearances.

Finally, Edwina decided business was slow enough she could shut up the diner early. She sent Jupiter home, locked the door behind him, taped a sign in the window, then headed out the back with the garbage. After that, she went straight to Virgil's. She needed to know what was going on and, if Virgil was missing, why hadn't David reported him?

Virgil and David lived a mere six blocks from Pink Lady Donuts in a cute little cottage that had been built sometime in the early twentieth century. The front yard was overflowing with blooms even this late in the season. The front porch was crowded with potted plants of every variety from herbs to succulents. A thick swath of wisteria had been trained up and over the porch roof. While it wasn't blooming, the leaves were still thick and lush.

She rapped briskly on the red front door. To anyone watching, she looked cool as a cucumber, but inside she was seething with impatience.

It seemed like forever, but at last the front door swung open and David stood there in rumpled, striped pajamas that looked like he'd worn them for days. His salt and pepper hair stood on end and his eyes were red rimmed. He'd clearly been crying.

"Edwina! What are you doing here?" Was that a flash of fear that flickered across his face? Hard to say. It was there and gone so fast.

She didn't love that response in people, although she could understand it and sometimes it made her job easier. Thanks to the witch council, Deepwood's supernatural citizens often viewed her as akin to the boogeyman. Which wasn't true, of course. Unless you broke the law, then yes, she would hunt your butt down and hand you over to be dealt with appropriately. Using magic to commit crimes was a no-go as far as the council was concerned. On that she agreed.

"Is Virgil here?"

He shook his head. "No. He didn't come home."

"Didn't come home when? How long has he been missing?"

He rubbed his eyes. "I'm not sure."

"Can I come in?" She didn't wait for an invite but pushed her way inside.

The door opened directly into the living room. It was small but cozy with an ivory-colored plush couch piled with colorful pillows and shelves overflowing with books. A box of Kleenex and several half empty mugs of tea sat on the coffee table, as if David had made it, drunk some, then forgot it was there. To her, that was a clear sign of someone who was upset.

"When was the last time you saw Virgil?"

"Um." He rubbed his eyes again. "Wednesday morning when he went to work."

"Anything unusual that morning?"

He shook his head. "I don't think so. I was still in bed. He gets up so early."

"Sure, I get that. So he got up and you stayed in bed. Then what?"

"I fell back asleep, but when I got up, he'd made coffee and left a post-it like usual."

"What did the post-it say?"

David gave a little smile. "That he loved me and to have a nice day."

That was sweet. Corny, but sweet. "Okay, so that was all his usual routine? Nothing weird?"

"No, nothing at all. He was his usual, cheerful self. He even sent a text to ask what I wanted for dinner. I told him I'd pick up Thai. It was... normal. Only he never came home."

That gave her pause. "Why didn't you call the police? Report him missing?"

"I did, but they told me he had to be missing for 48 hours. It's only just been 48 now. I was about to call them again when you knocked."

"Well hold off until I finish here. Maybe I'll find something."

He nodded albeit with an air of confusion and worry. "Of course. Thank you."

"Did you know he got in an argument with Flynn Faolan that afternoon?"

David blinked. "Seriously?"

Edwina nodded. "Charis told me. Flynn had to park in front of Pink Lady, and Virgil lit into him over it."

David frowned. "That's not like Virgil at all." He sank down on the couch. "Although, now you mention it, he was a little irritable Tuesday evening. I thought it was because he got a message from one of his suppliers that a shipment was delayed."

"Was his reaction unusual?"

"I didn't think so at the time, but now I'm not sure," he admitted.

"Would you mind if I looked around a bit?"

"Please. I'm really worried."

He seemed genuine, and she'd known David and Virgil long enough to know the two were devoted to each other. Then again, things changed. People grew apart. Could that be what happened? And David got rid of Virgil?

She really had to stop staying up late watching serial killer documentaries.

She stepped into the cottage's small kitchen and closed her eyes, inhaled deeply. She imagined a stream of purple light streaming from out in the universe down through the crown of her head, filling her with energy. It was how she centered herself, focused her power. She wasn't a particularly strong witch, magically speaking, but tracking was a special skill. When she opened herself to the magic, she could track a falcon on a cloudy day, to quote one of her favorite movies.

Through half-lidded eyes, she surveyed the room. Faint golden fingerprints appeared, glowing against white cupboard doors. Footprints passed back and forth over each other across the wood planked floor. Two sets. The only residual energies were those of peace, domesticity, and contentment. This was a happy place for Virgil and David, but she hadn't needed her magic to tell her that.

Then again, people changed…

She made her way through the rest of the small house with the same results. Whatever had happened to Virgil hadn't happened here.

"Thanks, David," she said when she'd finished. "You call the police, right? Ask for Chief Dekes. Tell him I told you to call."

"You didn't find anything, did you?" He slumped against the couch cushions. A round gold and purple pillow toppled onto the floor and rolled toward the fireplace. He didn't even notice.

"No, I didn't," she admitted. "But I will."

CHAPTER

FOUR

Despite it being late, Edwina headed straight to the police station.

The station was located in a brick building built around 1910, along with the town hall, jail, and the courts. Unfortunately—or fortunately, depending on your view—at some point someone had gotten confused, decided it was medieval times, and put a couple of unusually hideous gargoyles on the roof. Granted, gargoyles were supposed to be ugly, but these really took the cake.

"Just got off the phone with David Zante," Jeremiah said by way of greeting. "He's officially filed a missing person report for Virgil."

She nodded and plunked in the chair next to his desk. The office was utilitarian, much like the man. No fancy frills or framed awards, just a potted cactus on the desk. "I scanned their home. Nothing of interest."

He smoothed his moustache. "Too bad. Hopefully there's something at the bakery. I did look up the other missing persons you mentioned."

"And?"

"They were all shifters."

"I know," she said.

"What I mean is, Virgil isn't a shifter. Is he?"

"Not that I know of," she admitted. "We've always known he's something, but not a shifter."

He leaned back, steepling his fingers. "How do you know?"

42

She shrugged, not sure how to explain what she felt around shifters. "Energy's wrong."

He waited patiently, obviously wanting her to expand.

She sighed heavily. "I don't know how it is with other witches, but for me, I get around supernaturals and I... feel things."

"Like?" he prodded.

"Like... with other witches it's a warm zingy feeling. Sort of... zesty."

"Witches are zesty." His tone was dry, but his eyes sparkled with humor.

She rolled her eyes. "Their energy is. To me anyway. Sometimes I can even tell a witch's affinity. I once met a witch with an affinity for plants. She was zesty and green."

He snorted but covered it up with a cough. "Okay, zesty and green. Got it. What about other types of supernaturals?"

"I met a sidhe prince once. Don't recommend it. Hot and itchy."

His lips twitched. "That sounds unpleasant."

"It was. Worse than any hot flash, and I had plenty in my day. Vampires... taste like metal."

He choked.

"Not literally, you dufus," she snapped. "I'm not actually tasting them. But I get this sort of tang on the back of my tongue like when you sucked on pennies as a kid."

He eyed her. "Who the devil sucks on pennies?"

She ignored his comment. "Which brings us around to shifters."

"Fuzzy but in a way that makes the hairs stand up on the back of your neck. Like you're not sure if you want to pet them, run for the hills, or pee your pants."

He turned red and pressed a fist against his lips. "Fuzzy. Pee your pants. Got it. And Virgil fit none of those?"

She shook her head. "Nope. Most of the time he felt like a normal, non-magical human, but every now and then I'd get this zip of energy like he was... something. But I never felt anything like it before."

"And you didn't ask."

"Seemed rude. Like asking a woman her weight."

"Yeah, that's not a good life choice," he muttered.

She grinned and knew it was a bit feral. "Definitely not."

"I'll get David to let us into the shop," Jeremiah said. "And I'll get my people on tracking Virgil's movements. See if we can get a ping off his cell phone. Maybe David can tell us if his credit card has been used."

"Virgil didn't leave of his own accord," she insisted.

"I don't doubt that, but we have to cover our bases. Besides, if someone took him, that person might be using his card or phone."

Of course. It made sense. "But you don't think it's connected to the missing shifters."

"I doubt it. Not if Virgil isn't one. Why would whoever is taking them — if anyone is — break their pattern now?"

He had a good point, but Edwina wasn't convinced. In fact, she was certain the full moon disappearances were connected. She just didn't know how or why.

Yet.

Edwina was glad she was on foot as it gave her a chance to use her Google Foo. Some witches used magic to ascertain information, but in her opinion, Googling was The Way. Besides, it took less energy.

She wasn't entirely sure what she was looking for, but she knew she would know it when she saw it. And see it she did.

It wasn't just shifters that were disappearing around the time of the full moon, but other things had been happening, too. For the last six months, the full moon had always been marked by strange and criminal occurrences.

The first event had been in March. A warehouse on the edge of town had burned down. Arson, according to the fire chief, but the owners had an alibi and there hadn't been any evidence other than a few cans of spray paint and some empty beer bottles. Kids having a party, the owners pointed out. Eventually the insurance had paid out a cool million.

Since then, there'd been a couple of robberies (one was a liquor store flush with cash, and the other a crystal shop of all things), some property damage, a carjacking. The crimes didn't feel connected in any way except for the fact they all occurred on full moons, and they all involved a nice chunk of change. Even the crystal shop. Apparently, they'd had a shipment of painite in. Metaphysically it was good for opening chakras, healing, and pain relief. Didn't seem like much of a thing except it was worth a whopping sixty grand per carat. Thanks to a special order from the largest local coven, the shop had been holding a couple carats of product. Unlike diamond necklaces or emerald rings, painite wasn't exactly traceable, and the small size of the crystal made it easy to transport.

Then there was the carjacking. Three, actually. They had all been Priuses. Which seemed ridiculous until she discovered that catalytic converters were being stolen willy-nilly for their precious metals, and Priuses had the most metal of all the catalytic converters, making them the most valuable. Forget

Lamborghinis and Porsches. Priuses were the new gold on the streets.

So money and the moon. Those were the things connecting these crimes. Which didn't mean much, but it made the hair on the nape of her neck rise.

What, if anything, it had to do with shifters disappearing was beyond her. She was going to need to bring in the big guns.

She pulled out her phone and swiped through her contacts. A voice answered on the second ring.

"Edwina? Everything okay?"

"You still up? I've got a witchy emergency."

Crystals, Cauldrons, and Crime

CHAPTER

FIVE

It was just past 11:00 p.m. when Edwina knocked on Emory Chastain's door. Emory lived in a rambling old Victorian a few blocks from Main Street where the shops were located, including Emory's own, Healing Herbs, which was practically across the street from Pink Lady. Primo spot in Edwina's opinion.

The door swung open, and Veri stood there dressed in a flowing leopard print and gold caftan, her hair done up in a matching head wrap. Gold-painted toenails peeped from her kitten-heeled black mules. Edwina wasn't sure if it was a going to bed or watching Golden Girls outfit.

"Didn't expect you." Edwina entered the front hall, automatically wiping her boots on the Witch Please doormat. "Did Emory wake the whole neighborhood?"

"She said it was an emergency," Veri said as if that was all that mattered. "When our sisters call, we come."

"Thanks," Edwina muttered. She supposed that was the upside of belonging to a coven. She usually had to rely on herself. Except that Emory and her coven kept inserting themselves into her investigations, insisting on "helping." Sometimes it was amusing. Sometimes annoying. She was certainly glad of it this time.

As usual, the coven had set up in the living room. The furniture had been shoved back and the carpet rolled up to reveal the pentagram painted on the floor beneath. Candles had been set at each of the four corners along with crystals of varying hues. A small cauldron sat in the center.

Also as usual, Lene was passing out freshly baked cookies. Edwina could still smell the scent of them lingering in the air. As well as an affinity for spells, Emory was an excellent baker and infused many of her baked goods with a hint of magic.

"Double chocolate peppermint," Lene said, offering her one. "For mental clarity and opening the third eye."

"Seems like the right thing for this," Edwina mumbled, selecting a cookie and taking a big bite. She wasn't sure if it clarified anything, but it sure was tasty.

"Okay, witches, gather 'round," Emory ordered, taking her place in the circle. "Edwina, you're in the center."

Edwina frowned as the other coven members stood at their respective corners. She usually sat these out. Watched from the sidelines. She didn't have the immense power these witches had, but Emory beckoned, and what Emory wanted, Emory got. At least when it came to magic. She might look like a thirty-year-old, but she'd been around since Prohibition. Veri was even older. She'd been around when Lizzie Borden went viral. Only Mia, Lene, and Edwina herself looked their actual ages.

"You sure about this?" she asked.

Emory gave her a stern look.

"Fine." She strode to the center of the circle and stared down at the cauldron. "What do I do with that?"

"Hold it," Emory said.

Edwina shrugged and picked it up. Although it was made of cast iron, the small pot wasn't much bigger than a cereal bowl. Inside was a gorgeous array of crystals: blue-green amazonite for connection to others, darker blue apatite to open the third eye and support lucid dreaming, purple amethyst and charoite for divine guidance and spiritual awareness, mossy green moldavite to cleanse the aura, green and purple striped fluorite for focus and clarity, and clear quartz crystal to aid in accomplishing goals. It was a witch's first aid kit for clarity and awakening.

Emory led them through the raising of the circle and the calling of the four corners, something Edwina had done hundreds of times, yet she never failed to get a rush from the power that surged through every participant.

Emory drew a wide circle around them with her athame, then chanted, "Guardians of the watchtowers of the East, power of air, I summon you. Witness our rites and guard this circle."

Lene was next. "Guardians of the watchtowers of the South, power of fire, I summon you. Witness our rites and guard this circle."

"Guardians of the watchtowers of the West, power of water, I summon you. Witness our rites and guard this circle," Veri intoned.

And last, Mia. "Guardians of the watchtowers of the North, power of earth, I summon you. Witness our rites and guard this circle."

Emory raised her arms. "We conceive this circle as a place of revelation and clarification. So mote it be."

"So mote it be," they all echoed.

Then they moved on to the ritual.

"Edwina, which crystal calls to you?" Emory asked.

Edwina frowned. They were all pretty in their own way. She closed her eyes and focused herself just like she would when she was tracking. She opened her eyes. The amethyst glowed softly, so she picked it up.

Emory nodded. "You can put down the cauldron. Now, hold the amethyst in the palm of your hand, focus on it, and repeat after me: I open my heart and mind to the clarity the universe has in store and my own innate psychic abilities."

Edwina wasn't sure she had any psychic abilities, but she did as Emory instructed, repeating the words. She could have sworn the crystal grew warmer in her hands.

"May my intuition reach its highest potential, and may this situation with Virgil become clear. I will listen to the guidance of the universe, to my inner knowing, and receive the truth. Guide me to Virgil Zante. Illuminate the path."

Once again, Edwina repeated the words. By now the crystal was nearly hot.

"As I will so mote it be," Emory intoned.

"As I will so mote it be." All the witches joined in this time.

Then each witch thanked the Guardians of their element and bid them farewell before Emory closed the circle. "May the circle be open, yet forever unbroken. Blessed be."

"Now what happens?" Edwina asked once they'd all resumed eating cookies.

Emory smiled. "Now we wait."

By the time Edwina tumbled into bed, it was nearly three in the morning. She sent Maisie a text letting her know she'd be in late, then crashed hard.

She found herself in a dark room, unable to make out much in the way of details. There was a window, yes, through which she could see a moon nearly full. Only it wasn't this month's full moon. It couldn't be because the tree outside the window was only just starting to bud, and the moon had an almost icy aura around it that always reminded her of winter and cold. Early spring, then.

A person dressed in voluminous white stood in the middle of the room. A low, moaning chant rose and fell. It was impossible to tell the gender of the person either from figure or voice. Nor was it possible to tell what sort of invocation they were making. She wasn't even sure they were speaking English.

What she did feel was a deep well of anger and frustration. A smear of darkness in their energy.

The chanting continued as the images changed before her, like the colored sand in those old picture frames that shifted and swirled when you tilted it to create different patterns. In front of her was a two-story Craftsman house that had seen better days. Its front porch sagged a bit, and the lawn was overgrown. The door opened and a man walked out. He was about Edwina's age, scruffy and ill-kempt. His gaze was glassy, and he walked past her almost like he was in a trance. He didn't even bother to close and lock the front door.

The image shifted and she was back in the dark room with the robed figure, yet this time the scruffy man was also in the room. He knelt in the middle of a circle drawn in chalk while the figure in white chanted—did they never shut up? —and traced symbols on the man's forehead.

This time she found herself outside a shop. The moon hung full and bright white in the sky. The scruffy man stood out front, still with that glassy look in his eyes. Suddenly, he threw back his head and howled. Then he shifted. Not his whole body, just his right arm. It turned muscular and hairy with long claws. A shifter of some kind.

He grasped the door handle and yanked the entire door clean off its hinges!

The beep of the alarm echoed, threatening to alert the police if he didn't enter the right code. Without even batting an eyelash, he ripped it out of the wall, severing it from the source. So much for security.

She followed him inside. Long glass cases lined the walls filled with shadowy objects. She expected him to smash and grab anything in reach. Instead, he went straight for the back room and to the safe door in the wall which he ripped off its hinges as if it was made of paper. Using his unshifted left hand, he grabbed a small pouch, shoved it in his pants pocket, then turned and shuffled toward the front of the store. On his way, he paused to smash a few things here or there, as if half-heartedly covering his tracks.

Once they reached the sidewalk, he kept going, but she paused and turned around. The sign read: The Mystic Stone. This must be the crystal shop that had been robbed. Which meant the painite crystals were in that pouch in his pants pocket.

It was clear whoever the chanting person was, they were using magic to control shifters to steal and commit other crimes for them. Question was, why hadn't the police figured out that no ordinary thief was responsible? Regular burglars didn't rip doors off hinges and security alarms out of walls.

Then again, ordinary humans tended to see what they wanted to see. They'd likely explained it away with crowbars or something. Even Jeremiah could have missed the signs. Easy to do if you weren't looking for them.

Once again, the image shifted, and they were back in the dark room. The shifter had returned to his fully human form and knelt once again on the hard floor. He pulled the pouch from his pocket and handed it to the figure in white.

The figure murmured something, and the shifter's head fell forward as if he were praying. Or sleeping. Then the white figure poured the contents of the pouch onto their open palm. Sure enough, the moon rays caught the crystals, sparkling blood red in the pale light.

The figure slipped the crystals back into the pouch and tucked it beneath their robes. When they brought their hand from beneath the white fabric, she gasped. For in their hand was a wickedly sharp knife.

Before she could say a word, the figure stepped forward, grasped the shifter's gray hair, pulled his head back, and slashed the knife across his throat. She was thankful it was dark enough she couldn't see his blood spray the walls, but she could see the streak of dark fluid marring the perfect white of the killer's robes.

The image changed one last time, and this time the man kneeling in the center of the floor was Virgil.

She jolted awake. Her heart hammered in her chest. She had no idea who the killer was or why they were using shifters to accomplish their goals, nor did she know why they'd taken Virgil who she knew wasn't a shifter.

What she did know was that she had to find them before it was too late.

Crystals, Cauldrons, and Crime

CHAPTER
SIX

It was the day of the full moon, and Edwina woke early despite her late night. The hard press of urgency wouldn't let her sleep. Tonight, Virgil would be forced to commit a crime and then he would die.

And why? For the greed of another.

She wished she knew who it was she'd seen in her vision, but no such luck. If wishes were unicorns, I'd be richer than Bezos.

Hoping against hope, she headed straight for The Pink Lady. Hope was dashed the minute she arrived. The store was still dark. No one had been there.

Pulling out her phone, she dialed David's number. She didn't much care if he were busy or still asleep. This was important.

David answered after several rings, his voice raw and exhausted.

"Sorry to wake you," she said, not particularly sorry at all, though she felt for the man. "But I need you to come down and let me into the shop." Yes, Jeremiah had said he'd arrange it, but there was no time to wait.

There was a pause. "Why?"

"Because this is likely where whoever took Virgil took him from. I need to see if I can track him."

"I'll be there in five." And he hung up.

She liked a person with purpose who didn't ask a bunch of stupid questions. David knew what had to be done and was willing to do it.

While she waited, she circled the shop, letting her inner sight scan the area around the building. There had been a lot of people coming and going, leaving traces of their energy behind. There was the trace of a woman worried about something and the angry traces of a male shifter. At some point last night, a witch had walked by. Not one of Emory's coven, but someone with only the lightest dusting of magic, a cheerful outlook, and a determined nature.

Around back near the dumpsters, she found traces of Virgil, though they were faded since it had been several days now since he walked this way. His energy was... yellow. A bright goldenrod that came from his happiness and open disposition. An open disposition that had likely gotten him in trouble.

She half expected to find traces of what had happened to him, but there were none. So perhaps this wasn't where they'd gotten to him.

A car pulled into the gravel drive and parked next to her. The door swung open, and David stepped out. "Find anything yet?"

She shook her head. "Nothing of any use."

His expression sagged, but he straightened his shoulders and marched to the back door. He quickly unlocked it, opened the door, punched the code into the alarm system, and stepped out of her way.

She nodded in approval. Definitely a smart man.

Interesting that the code was set though.

"Does anyone besides you and Virgil have that code?" she asked.

He shook his head. "Just the two of us."

While it was possible David was involved, she didn't believe it for a second. More likely the person who took Virgil was controlling his mind and had him set the code himself. Though why they would bother was beyond her. Maybe it was so ingrained in his nature he'd just done it despite being brainwashed or whatever.

"Want the lights on?" David's voice interrupted her thoughts.

"No, thanks. Easier to concentrate without the distraction." There was enough light coming through the front window, she could pick her way through the kitchen.

First she walked toward the main part of the shop and stood behind the counter like Virgil did every day. She could imagine him surveying his domain with satisfaction. Dozens upon dozens of imprints peppered every inch of space. So many she almost didn't catch the one she was looking for.

It was... strange, at once angry, muddy, determined. It tasted of fury and frustration. Smelled of desperation and desire. And looked like a smear of ugly. Definitely the person she'd seen in her dream. Or vision. Whatever it was.

The imprint came right up to the register and stopped in front of where Virgil had stood. They'd talked, probably for several minutes. The imprint was strong, so whoever it was had been putting out a lot of energy. Weaving a spell, perhaps? Or using their natural magical abilities? Either way, it was enough to leave a strong impression even three days later.

She shifted her attention to a second trail of the same energy as it came around the side of the counter and behind, joining and mixing with Virgil's. She was going to bet this was the point where Virgil came under the kidnapper's influence. Now the two trails joined and headed for the back door.

And that's where they stopped.

It was as if they'd poofed into the ether. Was it possible the kidnapper had opened a portal? Surely that wasn't possible.

The portalways were a collection of... well, wormholes were the best way to describe them.

They led from our world to multiple others in both time and space. A person could step through here in Deepwood and end up in Paris in the 1920s. A portal could only be opened by witches of a certain bloodline, and those were incredibly rare. Emory and those of her coven were the last remaining portal witches as far as Edwina knew. Whoever this person was, they were definitely not a witch, which meant they shouldn't be able to open a portal. Besides, there was no residual tinge of ozone, though she wasn't sure there would be after so long. Still, she was pretty well convinced it wasn't a portal.

Teleportation? Could it be that? That was rare magic indeed and took enormous amounts of energy. She'd read about it but never met anyone who could do it. Certainly not for any distance and not with a second person in tow.

Which left flight. Could the kidnapper themself be a shifter? There were shifters who could fly: dragons, firebirds, sphinxes. Although she had a hard time imagining any of them would use their fellow shifters to commit crimes. Dragons would just do it themselves. Firebirds couldn't be bothered. And sphinxes were so rare, she would have heard if there was one lurking around town.

"David, can you come inside and tell me if anything is missing or out of place?"

He nodded and flipped on the overhead lights, walking past her into the kitchen. He frowned as he looked around. "Everything's normal as far as I can tell. Nothing missing."

"What about the display case? Would it usually be empty?"

"There are often a few donuts left over at the end of the day. Sometimes he brings some home. Other times he boxes them up and takes them over to the retirement home."

Always thinking of others. That was the Virgil she knew.

Something caught her eye. A spot of something against the pristine white floor. Virgil kept an immaculate kitchen, which meant whatever it was didn't belong there. She leaned down and scooped up a small spindly flower, crushed almost beyond recognition.

"What's that?" David craned his neck to see.

"It's a flower of some kind." She said, frowning at the small piece of flora in her palm. She sniffed. It smelled faintly of apples. How unusual. It certainly didn't belong around here. In fact, she'd never seen anything quite like it.

"It couldn't have been here long. Virgil would have swept it up immediately. Must have blown in when we opened the door."

She shook her head. "Unlikely. This isn't native to the region. It's some kind of orchid, I think, which means the only way to grow it is indoors."

"Someone could have tracked it in on their shoe," he pointed out.

Which was likely exactly how it got there. But Virgil never let anyone back in the kitchen except David. And the person who'd taken him. The orchid definitely hadn't been at Virgil and David's, which meant...

"I think whoever took Virgil tracked this in," she said.

He paled. "Can it help you find him?"

"Maybe," she said. "It just might."

There was one place in Deepwood that might carry unusual orchids. The Greenhouse at Deepwood Manor sold pretty much any kind of plant a person could think of, including many of the magical variety. While non-magical people shopped there, it was particularly popular with witches. If someone in town owned a plant as unusual as the one she'd found, someone at The Greenhouse would probably know about it.

Deepwood Manor sat at the edge of town on several acres of land. The gorgeous—and enormous—Victorian was typical of the area and had been painted a lovely sage green with white and forest green trim. It had a wide, wraparound porch, more turrets and gables than it probably needed, and an attic that she had on good authority was haunted.

It was owned by the three Blackthorne sisters: Zinnia, Willow, and Poppy. All were in their mid to late forties and all had incredibly green thumbs. Green witches, to be sure, though Willow claimed she was more of a hedge witch. In any case, they did marvels with the natural world.

Behind the Victorian stretched numerous greenhouses containing everything from bromeliads to black bat flowers. And behind those were open fields overflowing with native plants and herbs.

This time of day, she knew the sisters would be in the large sage green barn that served as both a workshop and a storefront for their business, so she drove down the gravel road which curved around the house, and parked. Thanks to the warm day, the barn doors were wide open, letting in sunshine and fresh air. A white sign above the door read: The Greenhouse Nursery.

Poppy Blackthorne stood behind a long, white beadboard fronted counter, putting together a display of homemade soaps on an antique jadeite cake stand. Her fiery red hair was done up in a messy bun on the top of her head and her tongue stuck out a bit as she hummed to herself. Sounded like Take on Me. Peppy.

She glanced up, and her golden-brown eyes crinkled at the corners. "Hello, Edwina."

"Hey, there, Poppy. Got a bit of a mystery for you."

Her eyes brightened, and she brushed her hands off on her pink apron. "Do tell."

Edwina laid the mangled flower down on the counter. "You know what this is?"

"Of course. It's a ghost orchid. Native to Cuba and South Florida. Incredibly rare. If that was a test, you're going to have to try harder." Her laugh was airy and bright.

"Not a test. I just wanted to know if you carry it."

"Afraid not. It's really hard to grow. I think Willow tried a while back, but it just didn't thrive."

"Unusual. I thought Willow could grow anything."

Poppy grinned. "Close, but not quite."

"Do you know of anyone in Deepwood who has it?"

Poppy hummed in thought. "I don't, but Willow definitely would. She's out in greenhouse five."

"Thanks." Edwina let Poppy get back to her arranging and exited the barn.

Greenhouse five was in the second row of greenhouses. She tromped between one and two. As she approached five, the sounds of salsa music drifted from within. She stepped inside and was immediately hit with scents of loamy earth and fresh green things.

Willow Blackthorne was in the middle of the greenhouse, bent over a workbench. Several pots were scattered around her, each filled with a small plant. She glanced up as Edwina drew near.

Edwina gave a little wave and tapped her ear. The music was loud enough there was no way they could converse. Willow lifted a remote, and the music immediately turned from a loud blast to a dull roar. Better.

"Edwina, what brings you out here?" Willow swiped a lock of dirty blonde hair out of her eyes. Dirt encrusted her fingernails and the lines of her hands. She didn't believe in gloves. She'd said more than once she liked to feel the earth beneath her fingers.

"Ghost orchid." She handed Willow the crushed flower.

Willow grimaced as she cradled the bloom in her hand. "Ugh. One of my few failures. I don't know what I'm doing wrong, but I can't get it to thrive." Her expression grew determined. "Yet." She handed the orchid back to Edwina.

"You have any on site?"

"Not at the moment. The last plant died. I'm waiting on a new order. Why?"

Edwina explained how Virgil had gone missing and that her only clue was a bit of plant matter left behind. Probably by his kidnapper. She didn't explain why he'd been kidnapped or the fact he'd probably end up dead if she didn't find him before tonight's full moon.

"Oh, that's terrible. Poor Virgil. He's such a nice man. And I love his margarita donuts. Let's see..." She leaned a hip against the table. "Vanessa Plum had one forever and a day ago. That's how I got my original clipping. I don't know what she did to keep that thing alive, but she did. For years. Of course, she's passed to the Otherside now, and the poor plant went with her. Not literally, of course, but it gave up the ghost right after. Nothing I did could save it. I could almost swear it was sentient."

Vanessa Plum had been one hundred and three when she died two years ago. There was no way she had anything to do with Virgil going missing.

"Anyone else?" Edwina asked.

"Remember Old Man Olsen?"

"Sure." Henrick Olsen — known universally as Old Man Olsen — had been a cantankerous old coot. Rich as Midas and stingy as Scrooge. She'd met him. Couldn't say she'd enjoyed the event. He'd been a misogynist to the core.

"Rumor has it his conservatory was full of rare and exotic plants. He could have had a ghost orchid for all I know, but he died, what, ten years ago? His place has been empty ever since. There's no way if he had a ghost orchid it would have survived all this time. They need a lot of pampering." She shrugged. "I'm afraid that's it. Sorry I couldn't have been more help."

"Thanks for trying," Edwina said.

Truth was, Willow had been a great help. Because what better place for a criminal to hide than Old Man Olsen's abandoned house?

As to the ghost orchid... well, who knew. Stranger things had happened than a rare and delicate plant surviving on its own for ten years. It was all she had to go on.

CHAPTER

SEVEN

Old Man Olsen had lived in a rambling old Spanish Mission Revival overlooking the Willamette River a couple miles out of Deepwood. Totally out of place in the rainy Pacific Northwest, but it was beautiful, nonetheless. It had likely once had a great view across the water to the treelined slopes beyond but, at some point, somebody had decided to throw up an interstate – and with it came the usual billboards, lighting, and so forth. Within Deepwood's peaceful borders, the interstate was hidden from view as it curved west away from the river, but here there was a splendid view right onto six lanes of asphalt.

Much like Deepwood Manor, there was a long, winding gravel road, only this one stopped in front of the house and had more dandelions than gravel. There was enough space to park at least four cars, but it was currently empty. The windows and doors were boarded up, and the property had an air of gloom and abandonment.

Edwina pulled her ancient SUV to the edge of the parking area, hood pointed toward the road just in case she had to move in a hurry. She debated leaving it unlocked for the same reason, then decided she'd better not. Yes, it took time to manually unlock a car door without a fob — the one time she regretted not having a newer model vehicle — but there was also the danger of someone getting into the car. She kept her key in hand and at the ready, just in case.

It was still light out, though it was evening and the shadows were growing long, so she picked her way along the side of the house. Looking for a chink in the armor, so to speak. The window she'd seen in her dream had been uncovered, as she'd had a clear view of the moon. Granted, she was no dreamwalker, so no telling how accurate her dream had been. But still, it seemed like a logical thing to look for.

The house was surrounded by waist-high grass and weeds that had mostly dried out over the summer. On the north side of the house, two narrow tracks had crushed it flat. Tire tracks. Recent. So someone had a vehicle here somewhere.

The tracks led to a dilapidated shed, half collapsed and weathered gray, which had formed a lean-to beneath a copse of overgrown evergreens. Sure enough, someone had parked a shiny new Mustang beneath the sloping roof. Brave of them. The place looked like it might collapse at any minute.

Although it was completely out of view of the driveway or the road beyond. Even from the river, the place would look abandoned should anyone bother to look.

Unfortunately, it was locked tight so she couldn't check registration. She snapped a photo of the vehicle and the license plate and sent it via text to Chief Dekes. Maybe he could figure out who it belonged to.

She carefully picked her way through the grasses to the house and circled around back. What had once probably been a lovely, landscaped area was now so overgrown it could rival Grey Gardens. Blackberry vines had overtaken everything, even trailing up and over the sagging back porch.

At the far corner of the house, she found it. A single, uncovered window. Based on its location, it would give an excellent view of the moon at night, and she was fairly sure that tree just to the side was the one she'd seen.

On the side of the house was the conservatory. Surprisingly, it was still intact despite no one having bothered to board it up. She supposed it would have been difficult to cover all those panes of glass.

She tested the door. Locked. But the lock was a cheap, flimsy thing, easily forced without much effort.

Inside, it stank of must and mildew. Green slime oozed down the glass panes, and the air was thick and close. Plants grew out of control, turning the conservatory into a literal jungle and plunging it into a perpetual twilight. How the heck were they still growing? She supposed without human interference, the place had become a self-contained terrarium, growing and flourishing with each passing year.

Something glowed white, and she stepped closer. There, twined around what looked like an enormous overgrown fern, was a ghost orchid.

This was it. This was where Virgil was being kept. She was certain.

Her phone vibrated in her pocket, and she pulled it out to a text from Jeremiah: WHERE ARE YOU?

She texted back: OLD MAN OLSON'S HOUSE.

There was a pause and then: WAIT FOR ME.

Looked like there was about to be a party.

"You're sure this is it?" Jeremiah Dekes eyeballed the derelict building with suspicion. They stood next to the lean-to where the Mustang was still parked.

She didn't blame him. It certainly didn't look like a hotbed of criminal activity. Twilight was close, plunging the place half into darkness. Definitely more haunted house than evil lair.

"Not sure of anything," she admitted. "I was going to go in and check, but you wanted me to wait."

"So you did?" He sounded surprised.

Not that she blamed him. She was a woman accustomed to doing precisely as she pleased. She couldn't explain why she'd done what he asked, only that something in her had told her she needed help.

"Don't sound so surprised," she said, unable to resist needling him a bit. "I'm a biddable woman."

He snorted.

"Why didn't you bring any of your people?" She'd expected a bunch of police cruisers to pull up. Instead, he'd arrived alone in his personal vehicle.

He shrugged. "Hard to explain to a bunch of non-magical people that we're going to bust into an abandoned house to rescue someone from an evil supernatural creature of unknown nature."

"Fair point."

"We're here!" Emory came puffing up, slightly out of breath, the rest of the coven trailing behind her. They'd parked down on the road as Edwina had asked and trudged through the overgrown terrain to convene at the lean-to. "Where should we set up?"

"What are they doing here?" Jeremiah muttered.

"We're going to need them," she said in a low voice. Louder she said, "We'll need to surround the property to ensure he or she doesn't escape." While rescuing Virgil was her number one priority, stopping the killer was high on her list as well. She wasn't about to let any more blood be spilled on her watch. Moonrise was at 8:30, so they didn't have a lot of time.

Emory nodded and then proceeded to direct her sister witches toward the four corners of the house. Each woman carried a bag of what Edwina considered magical goodies: crystals, candles, herbs, and whatnot.

Emory turned to her. "We'll raise the protection barrier from outside, that will prevent anyone escaping, but to keep stray magic in and boost the spell, you need to place this in the center of the house." She placed a large clear crystal about the size of her fist in Edwina's hand. "This is a Herkimer diamond."

"Aren't those stupid expensive?"

Emory grinned. "Very stupidly expensive. But they're also channels for energy. It will receive our spell and amplify it."

"Got it."

"And this is for you." Emory draped a silver chain around Edwina's neck. From it dangled a single black stone. "Jet to protect against violence."

Edwina had a feeling she'd need it.

"I've got one for you, too, Chief." Emory handed a chunk of jet to Dekes.

"Thanks." He tucked it in his shirt pocket.

"One last thing: here's the spell. Recite it once you've placed the stone." Emory handed Edwina a piece of paper then hurried to join the other witches.

"Ready?" Edwina asked, turning to Jeremiah.

He sighed. "As I'll ever be. Let's go play with magic."

"He's clearly taken up residence at the back of the house, so I suggest we go in the front." Edwina stared up at the impressive edifice. Most people would find it spooky or scary, but she was made of sterner stuff. Scary was facing down a man with a bomb strapped to his chest. Spooky was nearly having your life drained by a rogue incubus. This house was neither of those things.

Facing whoever was in the house was another matter.

They took the steps two at a time, and Jeremiah tested the boards nailed over the door. "These are loose. Like someone fixed them so they'd look immovable but swing aside easily."

"Clever," she said a bit dryly. "Door locked?"

He tested it. "Yeah."

Since her magic didn't exactly lean toward lock picking, she did it the old-fashioned way. The door opened smoothly without a single creak.

"Someone's oiled it recently," Jeremiah said, "or it would make a hellavua racket."

"I'd have left it unoiled."

"So nobody could sneak up on you." He winked.

The man was getting to know her a little too well. She wasn't sure she approved of the warm fuzzies it gave her.

It was almost pitch-black inside thanks to the plywood over the windows and the lateness of the hour. The only hint of light came from the open front door.

"Follow me," she whispered and headed for the center of the house. As far as she could tell, that was the study off the main hall. It was crammed with furniture draped in sheets that turned them ghostly.

Jeremiah checked his watch. "Two minutes."

Edwina tried not to fidget. She wasn't the fidgeting sort, but the longer they waited, the more likely they were to get caught by the kidnapper/killer. And the greater the chance Virgil might meet an untimely end.

She strode to what she assumed was the center of the room and placed the Herkimer diamond on the floor. She waited until Jeremiah gave her a nod, then recited the spell Emory had given her.

Nothing changed visually, but she felt a whoosh of power as it blasted upward. She could almost imagine the energies connecting, channeling through the crystal and creating a barrier that would keep anything bad inside. Hopefully.

"Let's go find this bastard," she muttered, striding toward the stairs.

Jeremiah followed along behind. Although he'd no doubt prefer to go first, only a very stupid man would have done so. And Jeremiah wasn't a stupid man. Yes, they were facing a dangerous criminal, but it was a criminal of the supernatural persuasion. This was her wheelhouse.

Based on the location of the unboarded window, she turned left at the top of the stairs. The hall was dark and lined with doors, most of which stood open leading into empty rooms lit only by the flashlight app from her phone. Her destination was the last room on the right.

This time the door was closed, and she hesitated, pressing her ear to the door. The door was thick and heavy, the way they used to make them.

Still she could hear the faintest murmur of a voice. It rose and fell, almost like singing.

Or chanting.

Crap on a cracker, we're too late.

No. She was having none of that.

She cautiously tapped the doorknob with her finger. The faint buzz of energy nipped her skin. Nothing terrible, just the tiniest pinch. She turned to Jeremiah and kept her voice barely a breath. "The room is warded."

His expression was grim, and he cocked his head as if to say, "Now what?"

She took a deep breath and focused. Outside, the spell surrounded the house in a protective energy shield. Nothing could get out. The witches were like colorful pillars of light on the edge of her inner vision: purple for Emory, green for Veri, gold for Lene, and blue for Mia. Their magic twined together forming an unbreakable bond of sisterhood and power. And in the middle, shooting up to join them, was her own: white and brighter than she'd have imagined. Whatever they were doing was augmenting her own natural abilities.

Good to know.

She turned her attention to whoever was behind the door. She still couldn't see them — they'd masked themselves well — but their power was strong, tainted with wrongful death and cruel intent. Magic was neutral, neither good nor bad, but it could be twisted, tainted, and wielded for evil just as well as good. And whoever was behind that door was definitely not good.

Next to the magic wielder was another energy. One she recognized. Virgil. She was sure of it. The magic was like nothing she'd ever experienced before, and yet it was him. It smelled, tasted, felt like him.

She drew in a deep breath and shifted all her attention on the spell locking the door. She couldn't see it like she could see the magic of living things —

not something she could usually do but clearly something she'd been temporarily given by Emory through the spell — but she could feel the threads of energy twisting through the metal and wood. Her own magic was used to following twisted trails, so she sent it out in seeking tendrils to curl themselves around the darker spell, choking it off from the magic that fed it until it crumbled and died like an old vine.

With a nod of satisfaction, she twisted the knob, pushed open the door, and stepped through.

A blast of magical energy hit her square in the chest.

CHAPTER
EIGHT

"Edwina!" Jeremiah shouted.

"Stay back!" She managed to wave him off. A gun was no match for the magic her attacker wielded.

"Wise choice." The voice was a sibilant whisper without discernible gender. "You are no match for me."

"Good grief, it's like a bad sci-fi movie villain day up in here," she grumbled, heaving herself to a sitting position.

The killer hissed. Like a freaking snake. It was weird.

"Edwina, what are you doing?" Jeremiah muttered.

Good question, but she couldn't help the snark. Pain radiated from her chest where the jet stone hung, out across her shoulders and down her arms. She was pretty sure without the stone she'd be dead. Thank goodness for Emory and her witchy intuition.

The killer stood in shadow, swathed in white robes, a hood pulled up to hide their features. "That blast should have killed you."

Points to her for guessing right. "Would have, except I've got some powerful friends." She squinted in the dim light. A figure knelt on the floor. "Virgil, that you?"

"He can't answer," the killer hissed.

"Right, because you've got him under a spell," she guessed.

The killer chuckled, a cold, chilling sound. It made her nervous, and she didn't like being nervous.

"Why don't you let me see your face."

"Why?"

"I like to know who I'm dealing with."

The killer shrugged and removed the hood, revealing a very young face with a hint of peach fuzz shadowing a pale upper lip and jaw. Hardly more than a teenager. He should probably be at home studying, not out killing people.

"What's your name?" she demanded.

"You can call me Exon."

She snorted. "Like the gas station? That's the dumbest name I ever heard. You've been playing too much Dungeons and Dragons. You know that's not real, right?"

"Edwina!" Jeremiah hissed a warning.

Exon's jaw tightened, his eyes snapped, and he looked like he wanted to slit her throat. "Not like the gas station! I'm a mage! A freaking mage, alright?

Don't make fun of me!" His voice rose on a squeak, then cracked. He cleared his throat, making an obvious effort to calm himself. "My power is real enough, witch."

"You say witch like it's a bad thing."

"Witches are useless," he sneered. "Nothing compared to my power."

She decided to let that go for the moment. "Why are you doing this?"

"Doing what?" the kid taunted.

"I know you're kidnapping shifters, enthralling them, and sending them to do your bidding, then killing them. Why?"

"I'd say it's pretty obvious. Which part is confusing to you?" Exon sneered.

"Well, I get why you're enthralling them. Obviously, it's the only way to control them. The whole robbery thing... money. It's always money with the likes of you. Killing them covers your tracks."

"Smart for a witch." The tone was mocking.

"Doesn't take a genius to figure that out." She shoved herself to her feet, proud when she swayed only a little. That blast had really taken it out of her.

She glanced over her shoulder. Jeremiah was hidden behind the door, gun drawn, waiting for her signal. She was a little surprised he trusted her to handle it. Then again, he was well aware they were in her world now, and he didn't have any magic.

It was getting late. She could almost feel the moon pressing against the horizon. She needed to end this before it was too late for Virgil.

"Why shifters, though?" she asked, keeping Exon's attention on her. "You could have enthralled almost anyone, right?"

The killer shrugged. "Yes, but shifters are easy. Animal brains. Especially on the full moon. It's like they're mindless puppets to my magic. Plus they're strong, so there's not a bunch of time wasted trying to pick locks and safes and stuff. I just find a shifter I like and send out a spell. Takes a few hours to work, but it always does." He smirked.

She supposed that explained Virgil's irritation and the argument he'd had right before he disappeared. The spell had him acting out of character.

Virgil's huddled form swayed just a bit, as if he were struggling against the spell that bound him. Exon didn't notice since Virgil was behind him, and Edwina wanted to keep it that way. Clearly, Virgil wasn't as enthralled as Exon believed him to be. Either the spell was weakening, or Virgil was stronger than Exon realized. Either way, she hoped he'd break it soon.

"So it was all for monetary gain," she guessed.

He shrugged. "In case you haven't noticed, money rules the world."

She supposed he wasn't wrong, as far as it went, but he was forgetting a lot of important stuff in between. Like love. Caring. And friendship...

"Why not just get a job?"

He laughed. "Boooring! Why bother when I can make other people do the work for me?"

"I suppose you've got a point." The lazy little creep.

She could feel the energy of the coven moving closer. They'd left their posts at the corners, entered the building, and were coming up the stairs. They'd be here soon. Which was good. She had a bad feeling she wouldn't be able to take this one down on her own.

"One question," she said. "How did you manage to leave the donut shop without leaving a trace?"

He shrugged. "Easy enough. I used a blocking spell. Thought it might be fun to mess with you."

"You knew I'd be on your trail."

He nodded. "Of course. You're the council's lapdog."

She ignored the jab. He may have known about her, but he'd still never seen her coming. "It was an interesting plan. One problem, though." She shifted slightly to the right, so she was out of the line of sight of the doorway.

"What's that?" Exon crossed his arms, totally unconcerned about her and her ability to stop him.

The other witches had joined Jeremiah and were hiding behind the door, their energies focused on... on her. They were pouring their magic into her, turning her into a conduit. It filled her, making her fingers twitch and her scalp itch. It was like the pressure of holding your breath under water. Building...

Virgil shifted slightly. Silently.

Come on, Virgil.

"Virgil isn't a shifter."

Exon snorted. "Of course he is."

She shook her head. Her fingers burned. "Nope. He's something, but he's no shifter."

"But he is," Exon whined. "I can feel it in him."

"What you felt was something else. Not a shifter." She grinned. "Too bad. You lose."

With a roar, Virgil vaulted into the air, knocking Exon to the ground. The two men grappled, but Exon was younger, stronger. He blasted Virgil with magic, throwing him back and into the wall. Exon rose, stalking toward the fallen older man, hands raised for a killing blow.

"Behind you, boy," Edwina said.

Exon whirled.

Edwina released the magic that had been building inside her. The blast was white hot. It lifted Exon off his feet, spun him around, then slammed him to the floor. His head bounced. Hard.

Lights out.

"Come on out, Jeremiah," Edwina said, sinking to the floor, drained.

Jeremiah hurried forward, keeping his weapon at the ready until he was sure Exon was out for the count. Then he flipped the kid on his stomach and cuffed him.

"Let me," Emory said, kneeling beside Jeremiah. She placed her hands on the cuffs and whispered a few words. For a brief moment the cuffs glowed gold, then they were just normal looking cuffs again. She sat back. "There. As long as these are on him, his magic is bound. The council can remove it permanently."

Jeremiah lifted a brow. "They'll do that?"

"He's killed half a dozen shifters at least," Edwina said. "They'll strip him clean. He'll never use magic again."

Jeremiah nodded and climbed to his feet, striding over to where she still sat. He held a hand. "You okay?"

She wasn't too proud to take that hand. "I've been better," she said as he hefted her to her feet. "Feel like I could sleep a week."

"It's the magic," Emory said as she went to check on Virgil. "You had more flowing through you than most people can handle. You'll need time to recover."

"And cookies," Lene said from the doorway. "Lots of cookies."

"Not opposed to that," Edwina muttered.

"Gods above, I need a stiff drink," Virgil groaned.

Edwina let out a pent-up breath she hadn't realized she'd been holding. "You alright over there?"

"I'll recover," he said. "Thanks for coming to my rescue."

She laughed, glancing at the full moon as it slid up into the sky. Just in time. "I missed my donuts."

Edwina slept most of the next day. Probably for the best. The coven had insisted she and Jeremiah join them for Mabon, the celebration of the autumnal equinox. Although she'd have preferred to stay home and sleep some more, she couldn't resist the siren's call of a good witchy celebration.

Jeremiah picked her up looking particularly sexy in a snug pair of jeans and a casual blue blazer over a black tee-shirt. Total silver fox. "You sure about this, Edwina? Yesterday was a lot."

"Wouldn't miss it for the world. Emory assured me she'd put out a chaise lounge just for me."

He grinned. "Ah, you plan to lounge around like the lady of the manor."

"You bet. And you're playing butler. My cocktail glass better stay full."

He laughed.

She wasn't entirely joking.

The party in Emory's back yard was already in full swing when they arrived.

She was pleased to find Virgil there, looking none the worse for wear, David by his side. Noah, Emory's husband, manned the grill along with Mia. The two were having an impassioned argument over the correct doneness of hamburgers. As long as it didn't moo at her and there was cheese involved, Edwina didn't care.

Orange paper lanterns hung from the trees, and the fence and porch were swathed in garlands of autumnal leaves. Gourds clustered around pots of crimson mums while the long table was decorated with vases of rust-colored mums and cornhusk dolls.

"Here. We've got a nice spot all set up for you," Veri said, guiding her to a proper overstuffed armchair with an ottoman, pillows for her back, and even a cozy throw should she get cold. It was a bit over the top, but she was still too tired to argue. Veri handed her a glass of honeyed mead and a dessert plate with a single bacon topped maple bar.

Edwina glanced over at Virgil who threw her a grin. Cheeky man. She took a big bite and made a show of chewing it. He threw back his head and laughed.

Relief coursed through her. He was going to be okay. They all were.

After a feast of hamburgers, hot dogs, grilled corn, and various potluck casseroles, Noah started a mini bonfire in the firepit. They all jotted down their intentions for the coming months on bits of paper, then burned them in the flames, sending them like little bits of magic into the universe.

Edwina found herself staring into the flames. Virgil joined her.

"I wanted to thank you for what you did," he said after a stretch. "I know you risked your life for me. More than the others did."

She shrugged. "It's my job."

"And yet it's a choice you make every day to risk your life for others. Thank you."

Her cheeks heated from more than the fire. She never did much like thanks. She did what she did because it was right, not because she needed acknowledgement. "You're welcome. Glad you're okay." She paused. "Weird though."

"Because he thought I was a shifter?"

"Yep." She eyed him. "You're not."

"No," he admitted. "I'm not. Well, not entirely. My grandfather was."

She lifted a brow. "Really?"

"Sabretooth tiger."

Her jaw dropped. "You're kidding me."

"Nope. Last of his kind, far as I know. I carry the gene, but I can't shift."

Which would explain why she'd always sensed something in him and why Exon had mistaken him for a shifter. There was still a little magic in there somewhere. "Is that why you were able to break his spell? Because you can't shift?"

He shrugged. "That's what I'm guessing. That and sabretooth shifters are... different than your usual shifter. Stronger. Wilder. And it gives me an almost magical ability with baked goods. No idea why." He snorted. "Animal brain my backside."

"He'll never harm anyone else as long as he lives," she assured him.

"Good. He's harmed too many already."

"You'll be okay though?" It had been a traumatic day, and Virgil had always struck her as a gentle man.

He nodded. "I've got David, and I've got my donuts. That's really all a man can ask for." His look of pure peace told her that was true. David and donuts were all he needed to be happy.

Speaking of happy...

Someone had put on some music. Emory and Noah had started the dancing. The rest not far behind.

Virgil went to find David, leaving Edwina alone by the fire. But not for long. Jeremiah appeared at her side, munching the last bite of one of Virgil's donuts.

"A dance, my lady?"

She glanced at the couples swirling around the grassy dance floor. "Don't mind if I do."

After all, dancing under a Mabon moon was its own kind of magic.

The End

Crystals, Cauldrons, and Crime

A Note from Shéa MacLeod

Thank you for reading. If you enjoyed this book, I'd appreciate it if you'd help others find it so they can enjoy it too.

Please return to the site where you purchased this book and leave a review to let other potential readers know what you liked or didn't like about the story.

Book updates can be found at www.sheamacleod.com

Be sure to sign up for my mailing list, so you don't miss out! https://www.subscribepage.com/cozymystery

You can follow me on Facebook https://www.facebook.com/sheamacleodcozymysteries or on Instagram under @SheaMacLeod_Author. You can also find me on my website: https://www.sheamacleod.com.

About Shéa MacLeod

Shéa MacLeod is the author of the Lady Rample Mysteries, the popular historical cozy mystery series set in 1930s London. She's also written paranormal romance and mysteries, urban fantasy, and contemporary romances with a splash of humor. She resides in the leafy green hills outside Portland, Oregon, where she indulges her fondness for strong coffee, Murder, She Wrote reruns, cocktails, and dragons.

Because everything's better with dragons.

Crystals, Cauldrons, and Crime

Other Cozy Mysteries by Shéa MacLeod

Deepwood Witches Mysteries
Potions, Poisons, and Peril
Wisteria, Witchery, and Woe
Moonlight, Magic, and Murder
Dreams, Divination, and Danger
Alchemy, Arsenic, and Alibis
Crystals, Cauldrons, and Crime

Season of the Witch
(A Paranormal Women's Fiction Cozy Mystery Series)
Lifestyles of the Witch and Ageless
In Charm's Way
Witchmas Spirits
Battle of the Hexes (coming soon)

Sugar Martin Vintage Cozy Mysteries
A Death in Devon
A Grave Gala
A Christmas Caper
A Riviera Rendezvous

Lady Rample Mysteries
Lady Rample Steps Out
Lady Rample Spies a Clue
Lady Rample and the Silver Screen
Lady Rample Sits In
Lady Rample and the Ghost of Christmas Past
Lady Rample and Cupid's Kiss
Lady Rample and the Mysterious Mr. Singh
Lady Rample and the Haunted Manor
Lady Rample and the Parisian Affair
Lady Rample and the Yuletide Caper

Lady Rample and the Mystery at the Museum (coming soon)

Made in the USA
Las Vegas, NV
08 September 2022

54852284R00073